The Pilgrim's Progress has been printed, read and translated more often than any book other than the Bible. People of all ages have found delight in the simple, earnest story of Christian, the Pilgrim. The events seem lifelike, following each other rapidly and consistently.

John Bunyan was born in 1628 in the village of Elstow, England. His father was a tinker, a lowly occupation. Nevertheless, his father sent him to school, to learn to read and write.

In 1674 Bunyan married an orphan who was a praying Christian. She led her husband to the Lord, and he was baptized. Bunyan soon began to preach but was arrested and thrown into prison for preaching without receiving permission from the established church. He remained there for twelve years, during which time he wrote this book.

The reading of *The Pilgrim's Progress* is not only a pleasurable experience, but a life-changing one as well.

THE PILGRIM'S PROGRESS

John Bunyan

A Modern Abridgement

BARBOUR
PUBLISHING, INC.
Uhrichsville, Ohio

ISBN 1-55748-812-6

Published by Barbour Publishing, Inc., P.O. Box 719, Uhrichsville, OH 44683 http://www.barbourbooks.com

 Member of the
Evangelical Christian
Publishers Association

Printed in the United States of America.

A man clothed in rags and weighed down by a great burden on his back stood facing away from his own house. He opened the Bible he held in his hand and as he read, he wept and trembled. Finally, no longer able to contain himself, he cried, "What shall I do?"

In this plight he entered his home and spoke his mind. "Oh, dear wife and children, I am distressed by this burden upon my back. Moreover, I am certain our city will be burned by fire from heaven. We shall all perish unless I find a way for us to escape."

His family was amazed—not because they thought what he said was true, but because they thought he was out of his head. He withdrew, often alone in the fields, to pray for them and read his Bible. For some days he spent his time this way.

One day he stood in the fields and cried, "What must I do to be saved?" He looked this way and that way as if he would run, but knew not where.

A man approached. "I am Evangelist. Why are you crying so?"

The man answered, "Sir, I read in this Bible that I am condemned to die, and after that to come to judgment. I find that I am not willing to do the first, nor able to do the second."

Evangelist asked, "Why are you not willing to die, since this life is so full of evil?"

The man answered, "I fear that this burden on my back will sink me to hell. I am not ready to go to judgment."

"Why then are you standing still?"

"I don't know where to go!"

"Read this." Evangelist gave him a roll of parchment that said, "Fly from the wrath to come."

Evangelist pointed beyond a wide plain. "Do you see the distant wicket gate?"

"No."

"Do you see the distant shining light?"

"I think I do."

So the man began to run. Seeing him, his wife and children cried after him to return. But the man put his fingers in his ears and ran on, crying, "Life! Life! Eternal life!"

Two neighbors, Obstinate and Pliable, overtook him, persuading him to return with them.

He answered, "You dwell in the City of Destruction. And dying there, you will sink into a place that burns with fire and brimstone. Come along with me."

"What!" said Obstinate. "And leave friends and comforts behind?"

"Yes," answered Christian, for that was now the man's name. "Those are not worthy to be compared with what I seek. I seek an inheritance incorruptible, undefiled, that never fades away. It awaits in heaven, to be bestowed on those who diligently seek it. Read about it in my Bible."

"Phooey on your Bible," said Obstinate. "Will you go back with us or not?"

"No, because I have put my 'hand to the plow.' "

"Come, neighbor Pliable," said Obstinate, "let us go home without him."

Pliable hesitated. "If what good Christian says is true, the things he looks for are better than ours. My heart longs to go with him."

"I will be no companion of such misled fantasies," said Obstinate and turned back.

"Are you certain the words of your book are true?" asked Pliable.

"Yes, the Bible was made by He who cannot lie. There is an endless kingdom to inhabit, and everlasting life. We will be given crowns of glory and garments that will make us shine like the sun. There will be no more crying, no more sorrow. We shall be with seraphims, and cherubims, and creatures that will dazzle our eyes. We shall meet with tens of thousands that have gone before us, loving and holy, everyone walking in the sight of God—all well again, and clothed in the garment of immortality."

"But how can we share in that?"

"The Lord has recorded in this Bible," answered Christian, "that if we are willing to have it, He will bestow it on us freely."

"The hearing of this is enough to delight one's heart. Come, let us quicken our pace."

Because they were careless, however, they became mired in a bog in the midst of the plain called the Slough of Despond.

Christian struggled across the Slough of Despond toward the wicket gate, but he could not get out because of the burden on his back. A man approached from the other side.

"Why didn't you look for the steps?" asked the man.

"Fear followed me so hard, I fell in the Slough."

"I am Help." And Help plucked Christian out and bid him on his way, explaining, "The Slough of Despond cannot be mended so that travelers pass safely. It is the accumulation of scum and filth that continually runs from the conviction for sin. Because even though the sinner is awakened to his lost condition, fears and doubts and discouraging apprehensions still run from his soul and settle in the Slough. It is not the pleasure of the King that the Slough remain so bad. There are, by direction of the Lawgiver, certain good and substantial steps, placed evenly through the very midst of the Slough. Yet because of the filth the steps are hardly seen, or if they are, dizzy men fall by the side anyway."

Now Christian, walking across the plain, met Mr. Worldly Wiseman, who dwelt in Carnal

Policy, a very great town close to the City of Destruction. Worldly Wiseman had some inkling of Christian, because Christian's departure was already gossip in other places.

"Will you heed my counsel?" asked Worldly Wiseman.

"If it is good, I will."

"There is no more dangerous and troublesome way in the world, than that which Evangelist has directed you. Hear me, you will meet weariness, pain, hunger, peril, sword, lions, dragons, darkness, and in a word, death."

"But this burden on my back is more terrible to me. I don't care what I meet if I also meet deliverance from my burden."

"How did you get that burden?"

"By reading this Bible."

"I thought so. It has happened to other weak men too. Remedy is at hand. You will meet with safety, friendship, and content."

"Sir, which is the way to this honest man's house?"

"You must go to that mountain over there. The first house is his."

So Christian went out of his way to go to Legality's house. The burden seemed even heavier, and the mountain soon loomed over the path and burst flashes of fire. Christian quaked with fear. At the sight of Evangelist he blushed for shame.

"What are you doing here, Christian?" asked Evangelist.

"A gentleman showed me a better way, short and not so rife with difficulties as the one you sent me on."

"God said, 'My righteous one will live by faith. And if he shrinks back, I will not be pleased with him.' You have begun to reject the counsel of the Most High. You drew back your foot from the way of peace."

Christian fell down. "Woe is me!"

Evangelist took his hand. "The Lord says, 'Every sin and blasphemy will be forgiven.' So be not faithless, but believing."

Christian stood up, revived a little.

Evangelist went on, "Worldly Wiseman, who savors only the doctrine of this world, did three terrible things. First, he turned you from the way. Secondly, Worldly Wiseman disparaged the Cross to you. Thirdly, he sent you on the way to death."

Worldly Wiseman almost beguiled Christian

out of his salvation. This mountain was Mount Sinai. Evangelist called out to the heavens for confirmation.

In bursts of fire, words rumbled from the mountain: "All who rely on observing the law are under a curse, for it is written: 'Cursed is everyone who does not continue to do everything written in the Book of the Law.'"

"And no one is able to obey every law," explained Evangelist.

Christian hurried on, refusing to speak to anyone, and found the way again. In time he found the wicket gate. Over the small narrow gate was written: "Knock, and the door will be opened to you."

He knocked, saying: "May I now enter here? Will he within open to sorry me, though I have been an undeserving rebel? Then shall I not fail to sing his lasting praise on high."

A serious man came to the gate. "I am Goodwill. Who knocks? From where have you come? What do you want?"

"I am a poor burdened sinner. I come from the City of Destruction, but I am going to Celestial City, so that I might be delivered from the wrath to come. Are you willing to let me in?"

"With all my heart." Goodwill opened the narrow gate and yanked Christian inside.

"Why did you do that?" sputtered Christian.

"The devil Beelzebub shoots arrows at those who come to this gate, in the hope they die before they enter. Who directed you here?"

"Evangelist. He told me you would tell me what to do."

"I will teach you about the way you must go. Look before you. Do you see the narrow way? That is the way you must go. It was laid out by the patriarchs, prophets, Christ, and His apostles. It is as straight as a rule can make it."

"But, are there no turnings and windings by which a stranger might lose his way?"

"There are many ways, but only the right way is straight and narrow."

Christian went on until he came to a house. He knocked and called out, "I am going to the Celestial City. I was told at the gate that if I called here, the Interpreter would show me excellent things."

The door opened. A man said, "I am the Interpreter. Come in."

The Interpreter took him to a private room where a portrait hung on the wall. The very somber man in the picture had his eyes lifted to heaven, the Best of Books in his hand, and the Law of Truth written on his lips. The world was behind his back and a crown of gold hung over his head. The man seemed to plead with men.

"What does this mean?" asked Christian.

"This man is the only guide authorized by the Lord of the place where you are going. Take good heed. In your journey you will meet with some who pretend to lead you the right way, but their way leads to death."

"And what is the meaning of this?" asked Christian.

"This parlor is the heart of a man never sanctified by the grace of the Gospel. The dust is original sin and a lifetime of corruptions that pollute the man. The man who swept is the Law. The maiden who sprinkled water is the Gospel. The Law increased sin in the heart, for it does not give power to subdue it. The Gospel vanquished sin, and the heart is made clean, fit for the King of Glory to enter."

The Interpreter took Christian into another room where two children sat in chairs. The oldest child, Passion, was restless. The younger child, Patience, sat quietly. The Interpreter said they had been told to wait one year for their reward. Someone brought Passion a bag of treasure, which caused him to rejoice and scorn Patience. But the treasure became rags.

"Explain this to me," asked Christian.

"Passion is a figure for the men of this world who want everything now. Patience is a figure for the men who await that world which is yet to come. 'For what is seen is temporary, but what is unseen is eternal.' "

Then the Interpreter took Christian into a room where a fire was burning on one wall. A fiend stood by, constantly casting water on it. Yet the fire burned ever higher and hotter.

"What does this mean?" asked Christian.

"The fire is the work of grace wrought in your heart. The man trying to extinguish the fire is the devil. Come with me."

The Interpreter led him to the other side of the wall. A figure hidden from the other room constantly cast oil from a flask into the fire.

"What does this mean?" asked Christian.

"This is Christ, who constantly maintains the fire already begun in your heart with the oil of His grace. It is hard for the tempted to see how the work of grace is maintained in the heart."

A bold man approached and said, "Write down my name, Sir."

With that the bold man drew his sword, donned a helmet, and fiercely fought his way through the armed men at the door. Inside a pleasant voice sang: "Come in, come in; Eternal glory you shall win."

"I know the meaning of that," said Christian. "Let me get on the way."

"No," said the Interpreter. "Not until I have shown you more."

He led Christian into a very dark room, where a man sat in an iron cage. The man's eyes were lowered, his hands folded together, and he sighed as if heartbroken.

"Who are you?" asked Christian.

"I am a man of despair. I sinned against the light of the Word and the goodness of God. I have grieved the Spirit, and He is gone. I have so hardened my heart I cannot repent. Oh, eternity! Eternity!"

Christian said, "God, help me shun the cause of this man's misery. Is it not time for me to go?"

"Wait until I show you one thing more."

The Interpreter led Christian into another room. A man rose from a bed, trembling. The man said, "I dreamed that the heavens above were black, and it thundered and the lightning flashed. Suddenly a trumpet blasted. In flaming fire was a man on a cloud, attended by thousands. A voice said, 'Arise, you dead. Come to judgment.' The man on the cloud opened a book. A voice cried, 'Gather together the tares, the chaff, and the stubble. Cast them into the burning lake.' A bottomless pit opened, emitting smoke and hideous noises. 'Gather my wheat into the barn,' cried the voice. Many people were carried away up to the clouds. But I was left behind! Then I woke up..."

"Have you considered these things?" the Interpreter asked Christian.

"Yes, and they put me in hope and fear."

So Christian went on his way, saying:

"Here I have seen things rare and
profitable,
Things pleasant, dreadful, things to
make me stable
In what I have begun to take in hand;
Then let me think on them, and understand
What it was they showed me, and let me be
Thankful, oh good Interpreter, to see."

The way was fenced on either side by a wall called Salvation. Christian ran, but not without great difficulty because of the burden on his back. He came to a rise and there stood a Cross, and below it a Sepulcher. Just as he came to the Cross, the burden fell from his back and tumbled into the mouth of the Sepulcher.

With a grateful heart, Christian said, "He has given me rest by His sorrow, and life by His death."

As he stood looking at the Cross and weeping, three Shining Ones came to him. "Peace be with you," they said. And one added, "Your sins are forgiven." Another stripped him of his rags and clothed him in an embroidered coat and other rich garments. The third put a mark on his forehead and gave him a rolled certificate with a seal. "Look at it as you go," said the Shining One, "and present it at the Celestial Gate."

Christian gave three leaps for joy and went on the way singing:

"How far I did come laden with my sin;
Nothing could ease the grief that I was in,
Until I came here: What a place is this!
Can this be the beginning of my bliss?
Is this where the burden falls from my back?
Can this be where the ropes of bondage crack?
Bless'd Cross! Bless'd Sepulcher! Blessed rather be
The Man who there was put to shame for me!"

∽

In a swale he saw three men fast asleep. Their ankles were chained. Christian cried, "Wake up and flee. I will help you take off your leg irons. The devil prowls like 'a roaring lion.' You will surely become prey for his teeth."

"I see no danger," said the one called Simple.

"After a little more sleep," answered the man called Sloth.

"Every tub must stand on its own bottom," said the third, Presumption. "Leave us alone."

And the men fell asleep again.

Christian went on. Soon, two men came tumbling over the wall onto the narrow way.

"We are Formalist and Hypocrisy," they said. "We were born in Vain-Glory and we are going to the Celestial City to get praise."

"Why didn't you come in at the gate? Don't you know that it is written: 'The man who does not enter...by the gate, but climbs in by some other way, is a thief and a robber'?"

They replied, "Don't trouble yourself. Our custom for more than a thousand years is to take a shortcut. We are on the way, just as you are. So why is your condition any better than ours?"

"I walk by the rule of my Master. You walk by the rude working of your own devices. You came in by yourselves, and you shall go out by yourselves—without His mercy."

He explained his rich garments, the mark on his forehead, and his rolled certificate with the seal. The two looked at each other and laughed. All three continued on the way. Soon they came to a spring at the foot of the Hill of Difficulty. Christian drank from the spring and saw that the narrow way went straight up the hill. Two other paths went around the base of the hill. One of the men took the path called Destruction. The other took the path called Danger.

Christian began to go up the hill, saying:

"This hill, though high, I do long to ascend,
To me the difficulty won't offend.
For I perceive the way to life lies here:
Come pluck up heart, let's neither faint nor
      fear;
Better, though difficult, the right way to go,
Than wrong, though easy, where the end is
      woe."

∽

As Christian ascended, he fell to clamber on his hands and knees because of the steepness. About halfway up was a pleasant arbor made by the Lord of the Hill for weary travelers. Christian sat down to rest and read his roll for comfort. Pleased, he fell asleep. The roll slipped from his hand.

He was startled from sleep by the proverb: "Go to the ant, you sluggard; consider its ways and be wise!"

Ashamed, he scrambled all the way to the top of the hill. Two men rushed toward him. "Sirs, why are you going the wrong way?" cried Christian.

"The farther we go, the more danger we meet with," said a man called Timorous.

"Before us were a couple of lions," said the other man, Mistrust. "If we came within their reach they would rip us to pieces."

"You make me afraid too," said Christian. "But going back to my own country is sure death. Going ahead is fear of death, and beyond it, everlasting life!"

Timorous and Mistrust scurried down the hill. And as Christian felt for his roll for comfort, he discovered it was gone. He fell on his knees and asked God to forgive him for his foolish sleeping. Then he went back to look for his roll, bewailing his sinful sleep, "Oh, what a wretch I am!"

Back at the arbor he spied his roll.

Who could know his joy at finding his rolled certificate? It was the assurance of his life, acceptance at the Celestial Gate. He thanked God for directing his eye to the roll.

Nevertheless, he went on his way, bewailing his bad fortune. Suddenly, he saw ahead a stately palace. It was beside the way. He rushed ahead, hoping to get lodging there. He entered a very narrow passage and saw the two lions just ahead. Now nothing but death was before him. He stopped. Should he go back?

Trembling, Christian went past the lions. Then he clapped his hands and ran to a gate on the way. "Sir, what palace is this?" he cried to the man who had yelled encouragement. "May I lodge here?"

"This Palace Beautiful was built by the Lord of the Hill for the relief and security of pilgrims," answered the man, who was the porter. "The sun is set. Why are you so late?"

After Christian recounted his foolishness in losing his roll, the porter said, "I will call out one of the Virgins. If she likes your talk, she will take you in to the rest of the family." He rang a bell.

Out came a beautiful but very serious maiden named Discretion. She asked him many questions. Finally, she smiled with tears in her eyes. She called out Prudence, Piety, and Charity. They, too, questioned him.

Piety asked, "What moved you at first to become a pilgrim?"

"The fear that unavoidable destruction awaited me." And Christian went on to describe his journey.

Then Prudence asked him, "Do you not yet bear some worldly desires?"

"Yes, but greatly against my will. My carnal

impulses are now my grief."

"What is it that makes you desire to go to the Celestial City?" asked Prudence.

"Why, I hope to see Him alive who did hang dead from the Cross. I hope to be rid of all those things in me that to this day are an annoyance. I am weary of my inner sickness. I long to be where I shall never die, with the company that shall continually cry, 'Holy, Holy, Holy is the Lord God Almighty.' "

Charity asked, "Aren't you a married man?"

"I have a wife and four boys." Weeping, Christian explained to Charity how hard he had tried to convince them to come with him on the way.

After that they sat down to a supper of rich food and fine wine. All their talk was about the Lord of the Hill. They saw Him as a great warrior who had fought and slain he who had the power of death. He did it with the loss of much blood. But that which put glory of grace into all that He did was that He did it from pure love. Some in the household said they had seen Him since He died on the Cross and no greater love of poor pilgrims was to be found from the east to the west. Thus they talked until late at night.

Christian slept in a large upper chamber of the Palace Beautiful called Peace.

In the morning he awoke to the rising sun and sang:

"Where am I now? Is this the love and care
Of Jesus; for the men that pilgrims are,
He did provide? That I should be forgiven,
And dwell already the next door to heaven!"

☙

His hosts next showed him rarities of the palace. In the study they showed him the pedigree of the Lord of the Hill, that He was the son of the ancient, from an eternal generation. Here also were recorded more fully the acts He had done, and the names of many hundreds He had taken into His service. Then they read some of the worthy acts His servants had done, how they had "conquered kingdoms, administered justice, and gained what was promised; who shut the mouths of lions, quenched the fury of the flames, and escaped the edge of the sword; whose weakness was turned to strength; and who became powerful in battle and routed foreign armies."

The next day they took him into the armory and showed all kinds of armor the Lord had provided for pilgrims: sword, shield, helmet, breastplate, enough to harness as many men for the service of the Lord as there are stars in the heavens. They also showed him Moses' rod, the trumpets with which Gideon put to flight the armies of Midian, the jawbone with which Samson fought, and the sling and stone with which David killed Goliath.

One morning when the day was clear, they took him to the top of the palace.

"Let us go again to the armory," they said. And there they harnessed him from head to foot with armor, to protect him should he meet with assaults on the way.

Thus equipped, Christian walked with his friends Discretion, Piety, Charity, and Prudence down the hill. "It appears to be as dangerous going down as it was coming up," he said.

"Yes," said Prudence. "It is hard for a man to go down into the Valley of Humiliation without tripping."

At the bottom of the hill his good companions gave him a loaf of bread, a bottle of wine, and a sack of raisins.

And Christian went his way.

Christian had gone but a little way in the Valley of Humiliation when he spied a fiend coming over the field to meet him. The monster was hideous to behold. Scaled like a fish, it had wings like a dragon and feet like a bear. Out of its belly came fire and smoke. Its mouth was fanged like a lion.

"Where do you come from? And where are you going?" demanded the monster.

"I come from the City of Destruction, which is a place of evil..."

"By this I perceive you are one of my subjects, for all that evil country is mine. I am Apollyon."

"I was born in your dominions, but your service was hard; 'for the wages of sin is death.' So I want to heal myself. I am going to the Celestial City."

"No prince will so lightly lose his subjects. Go back to the City of Destruction."

"I have given myself to the King of Princes."

"It is very common for those who have professed themselves His servants to return to me."

"I am His servant, and I will follow Him."

"Do you not know how many of His servants

have been put to shameful deaths!"

"That is glory to their account."

"You have already been unfaithful to Him. You almost choked in the Slough of Despond."

"All that is true, and much more. But the Prince I serve is merciful."

"Prepare to die," the monster raged.

Apollyon straddled the way. He threw a flaming spear. Christian blocked it with his shield. Then spears came as thick as hail. Christian had wounds on his head, hand, and foot. He backed up. The combat lasted half a day, Apollyon roaring hideously the whole time. Christian grew weaker and weaker. Sensing opportunity, Apollyon rushed Christian to wrestle him. Christian fell, losing his sword.

"I am sure of victory now," roared Apollyon.

Christian's groping hand found his sword. "Do not gloat over me, my enemy! Though I have fallen, I will rise." With that he gave Apollyon a deadly thrust, which made him stumble back. When the monster saw Christian ready to thrust again, he spread his wings and sped away.

Christian sang:

"Great Beelzebub, the captain of this fiend,
Designed my ruin; therefore to that end
He sent the fiend out harnessed, in a rage,
So hellish he did fiercely me engage:
But blessed Michael helped me, and I,
By dint of sword, did quickly make him fly:
To Michael's help, let me give lasting praise,
And thank, and bless his holy name always."

∽

Then came to him a hand with leaves from the Tree of Life. Christian applied them to his wounds, and they healed immediately. He ate the bread and drank the wine that had been given to him at the Palace Beautiful. Then, sword drawn, he left the valley to enter another: the Valley of the Shadow of Death!

Two men ran toward him. "Back! Back!" they cried. "If you prize either life or peace."

"What have you met with?" asked Christian.

"Why, the valley itself, which is dark as pitch. We also saw hobgoblins, satyrs, and dragons of the pit. We heard continual howling and yelling of people in unspeakable misery, bound in irons. Overhead hang clouds of confusion. Death hovers everywhere. It is dreadful—utter chaos."

But Christian went on. It was the way to his desired haven. On his right hand yawned a very deep ditch, into which the blind had led the blind for all ages.

Soon he came closer to flames and smoke shooting out in such abundance, with sparks and hideous screams, that his sword was no good now. He had another weapon: prayer. He cried, "I call 'on the name of the Lord: Oh Lord, save me!' "

Coming to a place where he thought he heard a pack of fiends creeping toward him, he stopped. He had half a thought to go back, but knew the danger of going back might be more than the danger of going forward. Yet the fiends came nearer and nearer.

He cried out in a fiery voice, "I will walk 'in the strength of the Lord!' "

The fiends disappeared.

After he passed the burning pit, he heard blasphemies behind him. Was it one of the wicked ones? He grieved to think the words might come from his own mind.

After some considerable time, he thought he heard a voice ahead: "Even though I walk through the Valley of the Shadow of Death, I fear no evil, for you are with me."

Christian calmed. Someone else who feared God was in this valley. And God was with him. When morning came, Christian looked back into the dark. He was deeply moved by his deliverance from such dangers. Yet, as the sun was rising, he could see the valley before him was, if possible, more dangerous. The way was full of snares, traps, and nets here, and full of pits and deep holes there. Had it been as dark as it had been the first part of the way, a thousand souls would have been lost there.

"His lamp shines upon my head, and by His light I walk through darkness."

In this light Christian came to the end of the valley.

Then he sang:

"Oh, world of wonders! (I can say no less)
That I should be preserved in the distress
That I have met with here! Oh, blessed be
The hand that from it has delivered me!
Dangers in darkness, devils, hell, and sin,
Surrounded me, while I was in this glen:
Yes! Snares and pits and traps and nets did
*   lie*

About my path, so worthless silly I
Might have been snared, entangled, and
    cast down:
But since I live, let Jesus wear the crown."

⌭

Now as Christian topped a small rise, he saw ahead of him a pilgrim.

Christian yelled, "Wait up and I will be your companion."

Faithful called back. "I cannot pause—the Avenger of Blood is behind me."

But Christian ran him down.

Faithful said, "There was much talk in town about your desperate journey, for that is what they call your pilgrimage. But I believed, and still do, fire and brimstone from above will destroy our city. Therefore, I made my escape."

"Did you hear no talk of neighbor Pliable?"

"He is seven times worse off than if he had never gone to the Slough of Despond. People mock and despise him as a turncoat!"

"Did you talk to him before you left?"

"He crosses the street to avoid me. He is ashamed of what he did."

" 'A dog returns to its vomit.' But let us leave

him. What have you met on the way?"

"I was sorely tempted by a woman named Wanton at the wicket gate, but I went my way. Then at the foot of the Hill of Difficulty I met an old man named Adam the First. He offered me his three daughters: Lust of the Flesh, Lust of the Eyes, and Pride of Life. And I was inclined to go until I saw written on his forehead: 'Put off the Old Man with his Deeds.' And it came burning into my mind that he was going to make me a slave. So when I refused and pulled away, he pinched me so hard I thought he had a piece of my flesh. When I got halfway up the Hill a man overtook me and beat me until I thought I was dead. He said he served Adam the First."

"That was Moses," said Christian. "He does not know how to show mercy to those who break the Law."

"Yes. He would doubtless have killed me, if someone had not stopped him."

"And who was that?"

"I did not know Him at first, but soon saw the holes in His hands and side. I was saved by the Lord of the Hill."

"Did you see the Palace Beautiful?"

"Yes, and the lions too, but they were asleep."

"Who did you meet in the Valley of Humiliation?" asked Christian.

"I met Discontent. He told me the valley was without honor. And if I were to wade through this valley I would offend all our friends: Pride, Arrogance, Self-Conceit, and Worldly-Glory. I told him they were indeed relatives of mine, for they are according to the flesh. But since I became a pilgrim, they disowned me. And I reject them."

"Who else did you meet?"

"Shame. He said Religion is a pitiful thing. Conscience is unmanly. Few of the mighty, rich, and wise were ever of my opinion. It is shameful to repent after a sermon. It is shameful to ask forgiveness for a petty fault. Religion alienates a man from the great."

"What did you say?"

"I said he only told me what men are. He told me nothing about God or the Word of God. And when I was rid of him, I sang:

"The trials that those pilgrims meet withal,
Who are obedient to the heavenly call,
Are many kinds and suited to the flesh,
And come, and come, and come again afresh.

So now, or some time else, we by them may
Be taken, overcome, and cast away.
Oh, let the pilgrims, those astride the way
Be vigilant, behave like saints today."

ᗡᑭ

"I'm glad you withstood the villain so bravely,"
said Christian. "Who else did you meet in the
valley?"

"No one. I had sunshine all the rest of the
way through the Valley of Humiliation, and also
through the Valley of the Shadow of Death."

The path became very wide and walking
beside them was a man who at first appeared tall
and handsome, yet became homelier the closer
he got to them.

"Are you going to the Heavenly Country?"
called Faithful.

"The same place," answered the man.

"May we have your good company? We will
talk of things that are profitable."

"Too many talk of things of no profit," answered the man. "What is so profitable as to
talk of things of God? And if a man loves to
talk of miracles, wonders, or signs, where shall
he find things so sweetly penned as in the Holy

Scripture?" The man talked on and on of being born again, the insufficiency of good works, and the need of faith.

"Indeed, few understand the necessity of a work of Grace in their soul, in order to gain eternal life, but live ignorantly in the works of the Law, by which no man can obtain the Kingdom of Heaven."

"By your leave," gushed Faithful. "Heavenly knowledge such as this is the gift of God." And Faithful whispered to Christian, "Surely this man will make a very excellent pilgrim!"

"Do you know him?" asked Christian.

"He is the son of Say-Well. His name is Talkative. He adapts to any company. He talks as well in a tavern. He has no religion in his heart or his home. They are as empty of religion as the white of an egg is of flavor. Religion is only on his tongue."

"Then I am greatly deceived."

"Remember: 'The Kingdom of God is not a matter of talk but of power.' Talkative is the shame of religion. He has caused many men to stumble and fall."

Said Faithful, "I am not fond of him now.

I know how to be rid of him." And Faithful called to Talkative, "How does the saving grace of God manifest itself, when it is in the heart of a man?"

"So we speak about the power of things? I'm happy to answer you. First, where the grace of God is in the heart it causes a great outcry against sin. Secondly..."

"Wait a moment," interrupted Faithful. "I think it shows itself by inclining the soul to abhor its sin."

"Why, what's the difference between crying out against sin and abhorring sin?"

"Oh, a great deal: A man may cry out because of a law against it, but he cannot abhor it unless he has a godly antipathy against it. What was your second point?"

"Great knowledge of the Gospel-Mysteries."

"That is also false. If a man 'can fathom all mysteries and all knowledge,' but has not love, he is nothing," countered Faithful. "What is another point?"

"None. I see we shall not agree."

Talkative flushed angrily. "You are not my judge. You are not fit to be talked to. Good-bye."

"Let him go," said Christian. "The loss is no

one's but his own."

Faithful said, "It may happen that he will think of it again."

"Men to whom religion is only a word make religion stink in the nostrils of many," said Christian. "I wish all such men could be dealt with as you have dealt with Talkative. Religion would enter their hearts, or the company of saints would be too hot for them."

Faithful sang:

"How Talkative at first lifts up his plumes!
How bravely does he speak. How he
  presumes
To overwhelm all minds near! But as soon
As I did speak of heart, like waning moon,
He shrivels to an ever smaller part:
And so do all, but those who know the
  heart."

Thus they talked of what they had seen on the way, and so made the way easy, instead of tedious. For now they went through wilderness. They were almost out of the wilderness when they saw someone coming after them.

"It is my good friend, Evangelist," said Christian.

"And mine too," said Faithful.

"Peace be with you, dearly beloved," called Evangelist, "and peace be with your helpers. How has it fared with you, my friends, since our last parting?"

Christian and Faithful told him of all things that had happened to them on the way.

"Right glad I am," said Evangelist, "that you have been victors. The day is coming when both he who sows and they who are reaped shall rejoice together. Hold fast. Let no man take your crown. You are not out of gunshot of Beelzebub."

Christian said, "We well know you are a prophet. Tell us what is going to happen to us."

"You must go through many tribulations to enter into the Kingdom of Heaven. You will soon come into a town and you will be beset with enemies who will strain hard to kill you. One or both of you will seal your testimony with blood. But be faithful unto death, and the King will give you the Crown of Life. He who shall die there will arrive at the Celestial

City sooner and escape many miseries of the rest of the journey."

Soon Christian and Faithful entered the town of Vanity. The town had kept a fair the year around for five thousand years, ever since Beelzebub and his legion had set up the fair because Vanity was on the way to the Celestial City. At the fair pilgrims could find houses, lands, trades, places, honors, titles, countries, kingdoms, lusts, pleasures, whores, blood, bodies, silver, gold, and pearls. To be seen were juggling, games, plays, fools, apes, knaves, and rogues. And for nothing there were murders, adulteries, cheats, and slanders.

Every pilgrim to the Celestial City had to go through this town. Even the Prince of Princes went through the town. Beelzebub would have made Him Lord of the Fair, would He have revered him as He went through the town. He was such a person of honor the devil showed Him all the kingdoms of the world. But the Blessed One left Vanity without spending one penny.

Christian and Faithful attracted intense interest. Their garments were like none other at the fair. They spoke of holy things, which no one at the fair could understand.

Word reached Beelzebub, who quickly had the men brought in for interrogation. Christian and Faithful said they were pilgrims going to their heavenly Jerusalem. The interrogators said the two were either madmen or troublemakers. They beat them and smeared them with dirt. They put them in a cage, so they would be a spectacle at the fair.

The two remained patient, giving good words for bad, kindness for injuries.

Some at the fair thought the men were treated unfairly and soon fights broke out among the merchants. The two poor men were beaten and marched in leg irons to terrorize the others. This time they were threatened with death.

Judge Hate-Good made Faithful the first prisoner of the Bar. At the trial three witnesses were sworn in: Envy, Superstition, and Opportunist. Envy testified, "This man is one of the vilest men in our country. He has no regard for prince or people, law or custom. He does all he can to persuade all men of his principles of faith and holiness. I heard him say Christianity and the customs of our town are diametrically opposite, and could not be reconciled. If any charge be lacking, I will be glad to enlarge my testimony against him."

Superstition testified, "I have no great acquaintance with this man, but I did hear him say that the people of Vanity worship in vain, are in sin, and shall be damned!"

"I have known this fellow for a long time," said Opportunist. "I have heard him rail not only against our noble Prince Beelzebub, but our prince's honorable friends Carnal-Delight, Luxurious, Vain-Glory, Lechery, and Greedy. He called you, Judge, an ungodly villain."

"Renegade! Heretic! Traitor!" yelled Judge Hate-Good. "Have you heard the charges by these honest gentlemen?"

"May I speak a few words in my defense?" asked Faithful.

"You will be slain immediately after the proceedings. Yet, so all men may see our gentleness to you, let us you hear what you have to say."

"In answer to Envy's charge, I only said that any prince or people or law or custom against the Word of God is also against Christianity. Lord, have mercy on me."

The Judge sent the jury out. In its chamber Blind-Man said, "I see clearly this man is a heretic." No-Good said, "Rid the earth of this fellow." "I hate the very looks of him," agreed Malice. Love-Lust added, "I could never endure him." Live-Loose said, "He would always be condemning my ways." "Hang him. Hang him," reasoned Brainy. High-Mind muttered, "A sorry scrub indeed." "My heart is black toward him," snarled Enmity. "He is a rogue," said Liar. Cruelty insisted, "Hanging is too good for him." Hate-Light said, "Let's get rid of him." Implacable had the final opinion, "Let's vote him guilty of death."

They therefore brought Faithful out to punish him according to their law. First, they scourged him. Then they beat him. Then they stabbed him with knives. After that they stoned him. Then they slashed him with swords. Then they burned him to ashes at the stake. Thus, Faithful died.

Unseen to the multitude, a chariot carried Faithful up through the clouds to the sound of trumpets and off to the Celestial Gate. And he who rules all things brought it about that Christian escaped his cage.

And Christian left Vanity mourning:

"Well, Faithful, you have faithfully professed
Unto your Lord, with Him you shall be
  blessed;
When faithless ones, with all their vain
  delights,
Are crying out under their hellish plights:
Sing, Faithful, sing, and let your name
  survive;
For though they killed you, yet are you alive."

∽

As Christian fled Vanity, he was joined by a man named Hopeful. And hopeful he was, made so by beholding the words and behavior of Christian and Faithful in their sufferings at the fair. Thus, one died testifying to the truth, another rose from his ashes to accompany Christian in his pilgrimage. Hopeful told Christian many more people at the fair would follow on the pilgrimage, but it would take time.

The two pilgrims soon overtook a man. "How far do you go this way? And where are you from?" they asked.

"I'm going to the Celestial City. I'm from the town of Fair-Speech. I have many rich relatives there. In particular Lord Turn-About, Lord Time-Server and Lord Fair-Speech himself. Also Smooth-Man, Facing-Both-Ways and Two-Tongues. And my wife is a very virtuous woman from a very honorable family. It's true we differ in religion from those of a stricter sort, yet only on two small points. First, we never strive against wind and tide. Secondly, we are most zealous when religion goes in his silver slippers. We love to walk with him in the street, if the sun shines and people applaud him."

Christian asked, "Is not your name By-Ends?"

"That is not my name. It is a nickname given to me by those who cannot stand me. I must be content to bear that reproach. I never gave an occasion to earn the name. I have always been lucky, that's all."

"If you go with us, you must go against wind and tide. And you must be loyal to religion in rags as well as silver slippers."

"You must not impose your faith," said By-Ends, "nor lord it over my faith. Let me go with you in freedom."

"Not a step further," said Christian.

"I won't desert my principles. I'll wait until someone comes along who will be glad of my company."

By-Ends asked innocently, "Suppose a minister or a tradesman had an opportunity to get the good blessings of life, but only if he had to become very zealous on some point of religion he never bothered with before. May he not get the blessings and still be an honorable man?"

Money-Love, who, along with Mr. Hold-the-World and Mr. Save-All, had followed Mr. By-Ends, spoke right away, "Let's take the minister first. If he can benefit from such a small alteration of principle, I see no reason why he can't do it and still be an honest man. After all, the desire for blessings is lawful and the opportunity is set before him by Providence. Besides, his desire makes him a more studious, a more zealous preacher. His people won't mind if he denies to serve them some of his principles. That will prove he has self-denying temperament. Now as to the tradesman, suppose such a one has a poor business, but by being religious, he can improve his market, maybe even get a rich wife. I see no reason why this is not lawful. To become religious is a virtue. Nor is it unlawful to get a rich wife. By becoming good himself, he gets a good wife and good customers and good profit." The others applauded Money-Love.

"What do you think, Christian?" asked Hold-the-World.

"A babe in religion could answer that. Only heathens, hypocrites, devils, and witches would make Christ and religion a stalking-horse to get worldly riches."

With that reprimand, the four men grew sullen and fell behind.

"If they cannot stand before a man, how will they stand before God?" asked Christian.

Christian and Hopeful crossed a plain called Ease to come to a hill called Lucre. A man called to them, "I am friend Demas. Come over here and I will show you a silver mine. With a little sweat, you may get rich."

"Let us go and see," said Hopeful.

"Not I," said Christian. "I have heard of this place. Many have fallen into the pit to be maimed or killed. The others are overcome by damp gas while digging." And he called to Demas, "Is not the place dangerous?"

"Only to those who are careless," answered Demas.

"You are an enemy to the righteous ways of the Lord, Demas," called Christian.

So Christian sang:

"By-Ends and Silver Demas both agree;
One calls, the other runs, that he may be
A partner in his Lucre, thus such fools
Are lost in this world, that the devil
*   rules."*

∽

The pilgrims came to a place where a monument stood by the side of the way. It seemed as if a woman had been transformed into a pillar. Written above the head were the words "Remember Lot's Wife."

Christian said, "This comes opportunely after the invitation from Demas."

"I am sorry I was so foolish. What difference is there between her sin and mine? Let grace be adored, and let me be ashamed. What a mercy it is that I myself was not made this example. She is a caution to both of us. We should thank God, fear him, and always 'Remember Lot's wife.' "

They reached a pleasant river. It seemed

David's River of God, John the Baptist's Water of Life. The pilgrims drank of the water. On both banks of the river were green trees with all kinds of fruit. On either side of the river was a meadow, beautified by lilies. Here they slept safely. When they awoke, they gathered fruit and drank the water of the river. This they did for several days and nights.

They sang:

> *"Behold you, how these crystal streams do glide*
> *To comfort pilgrims by the highway side.*
> *The meadows green besides their fragrant smell,*
> *Yield dainties for them: And he who can tell*
> *What pleasant fruits and leaves these trees do yield,*
> *Will soon sell all, so he can buy this field."*

℘

On the other side of a fence was By-Path Meadow. In the meadow a path went along the way. "Why shouldn't we walk over there?" asked Christian. "Come Hopeful, that path is easier going."

"But what if the path should lead us out of the way?"

"Does the path not parallel the way?" So they crossed a stile that spanned the fence and walked the path in the meadow. Ahead of them walked a man. Christian called, "Who are you? And where does this path go?"

"I'm Vain Confidence. This path goes to the Celestial City," replied the man.

"Didn't I tell you so?" Christian asked Hopeful.

At night they could no longer see the man ahead. But the pilgrims heard him fall, then heard only groaning.

"Has Vain Confidence fallen into a deep pit made by the prince of this world to catch over-confident fools?" asked Hopeful. "Let's stop." And it began to rain and thunder and lightning. Water began to rise around them.

A voice said, "Let your heart take you to the way again."

They slept, only to be awakened by a grim and surly voice. "I am Despair! You are trespassing my grounds of Doubting-Castle! You must come with me."

Despair was a giant!

He prodded them to his castle, where he threw them down into a very dark dungeon, nasty and stinking. Soon he was back. "My wife Diffidence counsels me to beat you without mercy." Without another word he cudgeled them fearfully.

They were very sore from the beating. "Why live?" asked Despair. "Life holds only bitterness. I'll give you a choice of a knife, a rope, or poison." But seized by a fit brought on by sunshine, he threw them back in the dungeon and withdrew.

Christian said, "The life we now live is miserable! My soul chooses strangling by rope rather than life."

"The Lord of the country to which we are going has said 'You shall not murder,' " replied Hopeful. "And for one to kill himself is to murder body and soul at once. And have you forgotten the hell that awaits murderers?" With that, Hopeful changed Christian's mind.

The next day Despair took them into the castle-yard and showed them bones and skulls of his victims. "These were pilgrims who trespassed on my grounds as you have done. I tore them into pieces. Within ten days I will tear you apart, just as I have done to these pilgrims before you." And he beat them all the way back into the dungeon.

From Wednesday morning until Saturday night Christian and Hopeful did not have one crumb of bread or drop of water. At midnight on Saturday they began to pray; they prayed until just before daybreak.

"What a fool I've been to lie in this stinking dungeon," said Christian to Hopeful. "I have a key in my bosom called Promise that is supposed to open any lock."

Christian used his key to unlock the door to the cell, then the door to the castle-yard, then the great iron gate to the castle. The gate creaked so loudly, Despair ran out in the sunshine to pursue them, but he was seized by a fit.

The men ran all the way back and found the stile that led to the way again. To prevent other pilgrims from making their mistake, they erected a pillar with a warning. That done, Christian and Hopeful continued on the way, singing:

"Out of the way we went, and then we found
What it was like to tread forbidden ground.
And let those who come after note today,

*Lest carelessness makes them, too, leave the
    way,
Lest they for trespassing, his prison bear,
Whose castle's Doubting, and whose name's
    Despair."*

ᔟ

They climbed up into the Delectable Mountains. They saw gardens and orchards, vineyards, and fountains of water. They drank and
washed themselves and freely ate of the vineyards. At the tops of the mountains by the way
four shepherds were feeding their flocks.

"Whose Delectable Mountains are these?"
asked Christian. "And whose sheep feed upon
them?"

"These mountains are Emmanuel's Land,"
answered a shepherd. "They are within sight of
His City. These sheep belong to Him; He laid
down His life for them."

"Is the way to the Celestial City safe or dangerous?" asked Christian.

"Safe for some. 'But the rebellious stumble'
in the way."

"Is there in this place any rest for the
weary?"

A shepherd replied, "The Lord of these mountains told us, 'Do not forget to entertain strangers.' "

Then the four shepherds asked Christian and Hopeful many questions.

"Welcome to the Delectable Mountains," said one. "We are Knowledge, Experience, Watchful, and Sincere."

The next day the shepherds took them to the top of the mountain called Error. The pilgrims looked down a precipice to see several men dashed to pieces.

"What happened?" asked Christian.

"These men listened to Hymenaeus and Philetus, who said the resurrection of the faithful had already taken place," answered a shepherd. "They lie unburied as a warning."

Next, they topped the mountain of Caution. In the distance they saw men stumbling, as if blind, among tombs. "What does this mean?" asked Christian.

A shepherd answered, "They are some of Despair's victims at Doubting-Castle. He rips out their eyes, and they wander to fulfill the proverb: A man who strays from the path of understanding comes to rest in the company of the dead."

Next, the shepherds led them into a valley where there was a door in the side of a mountain. As one shepherd opened the door, the odor of smoke and brimstone nearly overwhelmed them.

"What is it?" asked Christian.

"A detour to hell," answered a shepherd. "For hypocrites like Esau, who sold his birthright; or like Judas, who sold his Master; or like Alexander, who blasphemed the Gospel; or like the liars Ananias and Sapphira."

"Each one had started the pilgrimage like us," said Hopeful.

The shepherds walked them to the end of the mountains. On the mountain of Clear they let the pilgrims look toward the Celestial City through a telescope.

As they departed, one of the shepherds gave them a "Note of the Directions of the Way."

Another cautioned, "Beware of the Flatterer."

The third warned, "Take heed not to sleep on the Enchanted Ground."

The fourth bid them, "Godspeed!"

Then they went away, singing this song:

> *"Thus by the shepherds secrets are revealed,*
> *Which but for pilgrim eyes are kept*
>   *concealed:*
> *Come to the shepherds then, if serious*
> *To see things hidden, and mysterious."*

༶

Just beyond the mountains they entered a very dark lane. Off the way, they saw a man bound by seven strong cords to a pole carried by seven devils. They appeared to be walking back toward the detour to hell on the side of the mountain.

"The doomed man looks like Turn-Away from Apostasy," whispered Christian, trembling.

"Inscribed on the man's back are the words 'Wanton professor and damnable Apostate,' " whispered Hopeful.

Farther on, Christian said, "Let us pray we can do better. Even Peter, who said he could stand firmer for his Master than all other men, was foiled by the villains."

Farther on, a crooked lane joined the way. A youth had just briskly left that lane to walk the way.

"From what land do you come?" called Christian. "And where do you go?"

"I am Ignorance," replied the lad. "I come from Conceit. I'm going to the Celestial City."

"You may have some difficulty there getting in the Gate."

"As other good people do," answered Ignorance.

"But what rolled certificate do you have to show at the Gate?"

"I know my Lord's will," replied Ignorance. "I have lived a good life. I pay my debts. I pray, fast, pay tithes, give alms."

"But you didn't come in at the wicket gate," worried Christian. "I fear you will not get into the City. Instead you will be charged 'a thief and a robber.' "

"Be content to follow the religion of your country, and I will follow the religion of mine."

Christian whispered to Hopeful, "As Solomon the wise man says, 'Even as he walks along the road, the fool lacks sense and shows everyone how stupid he is.' Shall we talk further with him now or later?"

"Let us pass him and talk to him later, if he can bear it," said Hopeful.

A man in a white robe appeared on the other way.

"Where are you going?" he asked.

"To the Celestial City, but now we're not sure which is the right way," answered Christian.

"Follow me," said the man, "This is the way."

So they followed the man, who applauded everything the pilgrims said. Christian was confused. Did this new way ever so slowly depart from the way they had been on? Suddenly they were trapped inside a net. The white robe fell off the man. He was a devil. And the pilgrims knew they were being led to hell.

"Do you remember the proverb: 'Whoever flatters his neighbor is spreading a net for his feet?'" Christian asked Hopeful. "Did not the shepherds warn us about flatterers?"

"They also gave us a 'Note of the Directions of the Way,' which we forgot to read," lamented Hopeful.

They prayed for mercy. As they lay in the net a Shining One appeared, carrying a small whip. He asked where they came from and what they were doing there. They told him they were poor pilgrims on the way to the Celestial City. A devil in a white robe had tricked them out of the true way.

"It is Flatterer," said the Shining One. "He changes himself into an Angel of Light."

He ripped the net and led them back to the way. But before he left them, he whipped them severely and scolded them for forgetting the directions of the shepherds. As they continued on the right way, they sang:

> *"Now listen, you who walk along the way,*
> *To hear how pilgrims fare who go astray:*
> *Ensnared they were, entangled in a net,*
> *Because good counsel did the two forget.*
> *It's true one rescued them, but yet you see*
> *He whipped them too: Let this your caution*
>   *be."*

ᔪ

After a while they were met by a lone man. "Beware of another flatterer," whispered Hopeful.

"Where are you going?" asked the stranger.

"To the Celestial City," answered Christian.

The stranger laughed mightily. "What ignorant fellows you are, to take upon yourselves such a tedious journey. You'll get nothing for your pains, or my name isn't Atheist."

"Do you think we will not be received?"

"Received! There is no such place as you dream of. I have been seeking this City for twenty years."

"We walk in faith," chastised Hopeful. "We are not of those who shrink back and are destroyed, but of those who believe and are saved. We will go on."

They entered an easy land, but both soon became very drowsy. "Let's take a nap," yawned Hopeful.

"By no means, unless you never want to wake up again. Do you not remember the shepherd warning us of the Enchanted Ground?"

"Had I been here alone I might have died. The Wise Man said, 'Two are better than one.' "

Christian rhymed his advice:

"When saints grow sleepy, let them come to us,
And hear how lively pilgrims do discuss.
Yes, let them learn of what we did devise
To keep agape our drowsy, slumbering eyes;
Saints' fellowship if it be managed well,
Keeps them awake, and that in spite of hell."

"Where shall we begin our discussions?" asked Hopeful.

"Before the journey, what brought your sins to mind?"

"Many things brought my sins to mind: If I met a righteous man in the street. If anyone read the Bible. If I heard a neighbor was sick. If I heard the bell toll for the dead. If I heard of someone else's sudden death. If I thought I myself might come to sudden judgment."

"What did you do about it?" asked Hopeful.

"I endeavored to change my life. I prayed, read the Bible, wept for sin, and told the truth to my neighbors. But trouble returned."

"Why? Were you not reformed?"

"Because 'A man is not justified by Law, but by faith in Jesus Christ.' "

And one day in Vanity he had spoken his mind to Faithful. It was Faithful who taught him this prayer for salvation:

God be merciful to me a sinner, and make me to know and believe in Jesus Christ. For I see that if His righteousness had not been, or I have not faith in His righteousness, I will be utterly cast away. Lord, I have heard You are a merciful God, and have ordained Your Son Jesus Christ the Savior of the world. Moreover, I have heard You are willing to bestow on such a poor sinner as I Your grace in the salvation of my soul, through Your Son Jesus Christ. Amen.

∽

"Did you never again have doubts?" asked Christian.

"A hundred times twice told, until the Father showed me His Son. One day I saw Him—not with my eyes but with my heart. The Lord Jesus looked down from heaven on me, saying, 'Believe in the Lord Jesus, and you will be saved.' And I replied, 'Lord, I am a very great sinner.' He answered, 'My grace is sufficient for you.' And my heart was full of joy, my eyes full of tears, my love running over in the ways of Jesus Christ. If I had a thousand gallons of blood in my body, I could spill it all for the sake of the Lord Jesus."

Just then Hopeful looked back. "Look how far the youngster loiters behind us."

"Ignorance does not care for our company."

"Let's wait for him."

When Ignorance came closer, Christian yelled, "Why do you stay so far behind?"

"I take greater pleasure walking alone," replied Ignorance.

"What do you think of while you walk?"

"God and heaven."

"So do devils and damned souls," commented Christian.

"But I desire God and heaven," countered Ignorance.

"So do many who are never likely to go there. Why are you persuaded you have left everything for God and heaven?"

"My understanding tells me so," said Ignorance.

"The Wise Man says, 'He who trusts in himself is a fool.' "

And thus they bantered back and forth, Christian answering each of Ignorance's assumptions with truth from the Bible.

"This faith of yours is nowhere in the Bible. True faith takes refuge in Christ's righteousness, not your own."

"What! Would you have us trust to what Christ has done without us? You would have us sin all we want, because we may be justified by Christ's personal righteousness as long as we believe in it?"

"Ignorance is your name, and so you are," said Christian. "You are ignorant of the true effects of faith in this righteousness of Christ, which is to commit your heart to God in Christ and to love His ways."

"That is your faith, but not mine. I don't doubt mine is as good as yours," answered Ignorance. "I can't keep up with you. Go on ahead."

Christian and Hopeful chanted:

"Well, Ignorance, are you so foolish to
Reject good counsel, ten times given you?
And if you yet refuse it, you will know,
Too soon, the evil of your doing so.
Remember, man, in time: yield. Do not fear.
Good counsel taken well saves; therefore hear.
But if you yet reject it, you will be
The loser, Ignorance, we guarantee."

∽

Moments later, Christian asked, "What do you think of such men? Do they have no conviction of sin, and as a consequence no fear of their dangerous condition?"

"Sometimes they may be fearful."

"And yet they don't know that such conviction of sin and consequent fear tend to their good. They try to stifle their fear. But 'The fear of the Lord is the beginning of wisdom.' Did you know a man assertive in religion named Temporary?"

"Yes!" answered Hopeful. "He dwelt in Graceless, two miles from Honesty. He lived under the same roof as Turnback."

"Well, Temporary was awakened to his sins once. He even told me he was resolved to go on the pilgrimage. But after he grew acquainted with Save-Self, he became a stranger."

"He was a backslider," agreed Hopeless. "There were four reasons, I think. Although his conscience was awakened, his mind was unchanged. And he was held by the world; he didn't want to lose everything. A third reason was the shame he felt for religion. And lastly, he hated the feelings of guilt and hardened his heart. And now you tell me how a man backslides."

"They block all thoughts of God, death, and judgment. Then by degrees they cast off their private duties of prayers, curbing their lusts, ogling, and guilt. They shun the company of Christians. They cast off public duties of hearing, reading, and conferring. Then they begin to make fun of the godly, so they feel better about leaving religion." Christian went on to describe the final slide into the company of evil men and carnal pleasures, first secretly, and finally openly.

Suddenly the two pilgrims realized the Enchanted Ground was behind them.

"Beulah Land!"

The air was sweet and pleasant. Orchards, vineyards, and gardens opened their gates onto the way. "Whose goodly vineyards and gardens are these?" called the pilgrims to a gardener.

"They are the King's, planted here for His delight—and the solace of His pilgrims."

The gardener had them enter. They ate delicacies and strolled the King's walks and arbors. And they slept. The pilgrims relaxed and took solace there for many days.

The way went directly through Beulah. Beyond was the sight of the Celestial City. Some of its Shining Ones even came to walk in Beulah Land. It was in God's glory: 'as a bridegroom rejoices over his bride, so will God rejoice' over His pilgrims. Loud voices rumbled from the City: "See, your salvation comes!"

The pilgrims saw the City was built of pearls and precious stones. The streets were paved with gold. Reflections of sunbeams off the natural glory of the city made Christian sick with desire. Both he and Hopeful cried out, "If you see my Beloved, tell Him I am sick with love."

Finally the pilgrims no longer desired food or wine or sleep. They had to go on to the City. They could scarcely look at the City, the pure gold was so dazzlingly bright.

Two Shining Ones in golden robes met them.

Finally the Shining Ones said, "You have but two more difficulties and you are in the City. Come with us."

Between them and the Celestial Gate was a river. There was no bridge. "Is the river deep?" asked Christian.

"You will find it deeper or shallower, as you believe in the King of the City," was the answer.

The pilgrims entered the water. Christian began to sink. "The water is going over my head!"

"Be of good cheer, brother," said Hopeful. "I feel the bottom, and it is good."

"The sorrows of death have me, my friend. I shall not see the land that flows with milk and honey." Darkness and horror held Christian. He saw hobgoblins and evil spirits.

He was consumed with fear of death. Half

dead, he felt himself pulled upward by Hopeful.

"Brother, I see the Gate," encouraged Hopeful.

"You were always hopeful. But for my sins He has brought me into this trap and left me."

"You have quite forgotten the Bible," said Hopeful. The wicked 'have no struggles at their death...they are free from burdens' carried by good men. The troubles that you have in these waters are no sign that God has forsaken you, but are sent to test you. Will you call to mind His goodness that you received before today? Be of good cheer. Jesus Christ will make you whole!"

"Oh, I see Him now!" cried Christian. After that the hobgoblins and evil spirits were as silent as stones. He felt bottom. The river was shallow.

When they reached the far bank of the river, they were met by the two Shining Ones. They said, "We are ministering spirits sent forth to those who shall be heirs to salvation."

They sped upward, though the foundation upon which the City was grounded was higher than the clouds.

The Shining Ones said, "You are going now to the paradise of God. You will see the Tree of

Life and eat its imperishable fruit. You shall be given robes of light and you will walk and talk every day with the King, for all eternity. You will see no sorrow, no sickness, no affliction, no death. These former things have passed away. You are going now to Abraham, Isaac, and Jacob, and to the prophets."

"But what must we do in the Holy Place?" asked Christian.

"You shall receive comfort for all your toil, and joy for all your sorrow. You reap what you have sown, even the fruit of your prayers and tears. You must wear crowns of gold and enjoy the perpetual sight of the Holy One, for there you shall see Him as He is."

Now as they were drawing toward the Gate, they saw Ignorance already there.

"How can that be?" cried Christian.

"He crossed the river with no difficulty whatever," said the Shining Ones. "The ferryman Vain-Hope took him across."

Ignorance seemed agitated. He was alone. No one came out to meet him. Someone looked over from the top of the Gate. "What do you want?" the form asked Ignorance.

"I will eat and drink with the King."

"Where is your certificate?"

"I have none."

The two Shining Ones rushed to Ignorance, bound him hand and foot, and took him in a door lower on the hill.

"There is yet another detour to hell," gasped Christian, "even at the very Gate of heaven."

The Shining Ones returned to Christian and Hopeful. A throng of Heavenly Hosts came out to surround them.

The two Shining Ones said, "These are the men who have loved our Lord when they were in the world, and they have left all for His Holy Name."

The Heavenly Hosts gave a great shout and cried, "Blessed are those who are invited to the wedding supper of the Lamb!

"Blessed are they who do His commandments, that they may have the right to the Tree of Life, and may go through the Gate into the City."

After the Shining Ones instructed them, Christian and Hopeful cried to the Gate, "We call upon the Gatekeepers: Enoch, Moses, and Elijah."

Above the Gate three saints appeared.

"What do you want?" they asked.

"These pilgrims come from the City of Destruction," cried the Shining Ones, "for the love they bear to the King of this place."

"Bring their certificates," commanded a voice from above.

After their certificates were taken inside the Gate, those outside heard a cosmic voice, "Where are these men?" Then later the same voice boomed through the heavens, "Open the Gate that the righteous may enter, those who keep faith!"

All the bells in the City rang again for joy. Christian and Hopeful entered, to be transfigured, crowned with glory, and adorned in garments that made them shine like the sun. Hovering were seraphims, cherubims, and creatures too dazzling to recognize. And the whole Heavenly Host cried, 'Holy, Holy, Holy is the Lord God Almighty.' And Christian and Hopeful joined them in immortality to gaze upon the Holy One.

∽

Meanwhile, back in the City of Destruction, Christian's wife was in torment. Losing her husband had cost her many a tear. She remembered his restless groans, his tears, his burden.

Finally she said to her four boys, "Sons, I have sinned against your father. I would not go with him, and I have robbed you of everlasting life."

That night she dreamed. A parchment was unrolled before her, in which was recorded all her ways, and they were black indeed. She cried out, "Lord, have mercy on me, a sinner." Almost immediately two foul-looking creatures were beside her bed, saying, "What shall we do with this woman? If she continues this, we will lose her as surely as we lost her husband."

Next morning she awoke in a great sweat.

When there was a knock on the door, she called, "If you come in God's name, come in."

A man answered, "Amen." He opened the door and greeted her, "Peace be to this house. Do you know why I come? My name is Secret. I dwell with those on high. They tell me you are now aware of your sin. The Merciful One has sent me to tell you that He is a God ready to forgive, and that He takes delight the more pardons He gives. Here is a letter for you from the King."

She opened a perfumed letter. Letters of gold read: "I want you to come as your husband did on the way to the Celestial City, and dwell in my presence with joy forever."

"Oh, sir," she cried, "Won't you carry me and the boys with you, so that we may worship the King?"

"The bitter comes before the sweet," he answered. "Go to the wicket gate over beyond the plain, for that is the entrance to the way. Keep the letter with you. You must deliver it at the Celestial Gate."

The visitor left and she called the boys. "Let us pack and go to the Celestial City to live with your father in peace." The boys burst into tears of joy.

There was another knock on the door.

"If you come in God's name, come in," answered the wife of Christian, who now called herself Christiana. Two neighbors entered: Mrs. Timorous and the maiden, Mercy.

"Why are you packing?" asked Mrs. Timorous.

"To follow my good husband."

"For your children's sake, don't cast your-self away."

"They are going with me." Christiana went on to tell her everything, even reading the letter from the messenger.

"Oh, the madness that possesses you and your husband," replied Mrs. Timorous.

"The bitter comes before the sweet and makes the sweet even sweeter. Please leave. You did not come here in God's name."

"Come on, Mercy!" snapped Mrs. Timorous. "This fool scorns our counsel."

Mercy said, "Since this is Christiana's farewell, I will walk a little way with her."

Mrs. Timorous said, "I suspect you are thinking of going with her. Well, take heed: we are out of danger here in the City of Destruction. I can't wait to talk to Mrs. Bat's-Eyes, Mrs. Inconsiderate, Mrs. Light-Mind and Mrs. Know-Nothing. They know I'm right."

Christiana and the boys were soon on the way. Christiana said, "Cast your lot with us, Mercy. For I am sure not all the gold in Spain could make my husband sorry he is there in that place. You won't be rejected."

"But how do I know that?"

"Go with me to the wicket gate. See if you are allowed to enter."

"Lord, grant that my lot will fall with you," prayed Mercy. She began weeping. "My poor relatives remain in our sinful town, and there is no one to encourage them to come."

"Your leaving will encourage them, just as Christian's encouraged me."

"Let the most blessed be my guide,
If't be His blessed will,
Into His gate, into His fold,
Up to His Holy Hill.
And let Him gather those of mine,
Whom I have left behind."

Christiana knew from Pliable the Slough of Despond was where her husband almost smothered in mud, so she did not plunge straight in but found the steps.

The narrow gate was opened by a gatekeeper. "What do you want?" he asked.

Christiana said, "We want to be admitted through this gate to the way that leads to the Celestial City. I am Christiana, the wife of Christian."

"What?" marveled the keeper. "Are you

now a pilgrim, who once despised that life?" He waved her in and the boys too, saying, "Let the little children come to me." A trumpet sounded for joy.

Mercy blurted, "If there is any grace and forgiveness of sins to spare, please let me in too."

He gently led her in, "I take all who believe in to me, by whatever means they come to me."

Inside, all six pilgrims said they were sorry for their sins and begged his forgiveness. He told them that along the way they would see what deed saved them.

"Why do you keep such a cruel dog?" asked Mercy, still shaken.

"He belongs to Beelzebub, to frighten pilgrims from the way."

The pilgrims went on the way, between the walls of salvation. Suddenly Christiana saw the two foul-looking creatures she had seen in her dream. They came toward her as if to embrace her.

"Stand back or pass peaceably," she warned them.

"We want only to make women of you forever," they replied and tried to embrace Christiana and Mercy.

Christiana screamed, "Murder! Murder!" For she was sure they were fiends after body and soul.

"Would you make my Lord's people sin?" demanded a man who appeared on the way.

The two fiends jumped the wall and escaped into the realm of Beelzebub. They were seen joining the cruel mastiff.

"I marveled when you came in the gate that you did not ask our Lord for a protector," said the man.

"We felt so blessed we forgot all danger," said Christiana. "Should we go back and ask for one?"

"No. Go ahead. I will tell him of your confession. But remember: 'Ask and it will be given to you.' " And the man went back to the gate.

"I am to blame," said Christiana. "I was warned in a dream these two fiends would try to prevent my salvation."

Ahead they saw a house.

Christiana knocked on the door.

A maiden opened the door, "To whom do you wish to speak?"

"We understand this is a privileged place for pilgrims. I am Christiana, the wife of Christian, who some time ago traveled this way."

The maiden ran inside, yelling, "Christiana and her children are at the door!" The pilgrims heard rejoicing inside the house. Soon the master, the Interpreter, came to the door. "Come in, daughter of Abraham. Come, boys. Come, maiden Mercy."

Soon they saw all the things Christian had seen: the picture of Christ, the devil trying to extinguish grace, the man in the cage, and the rest.

"Is this the figure of the man of the world?" asked Christiana.

"Yes," said the Interpreter. "The rake is his carnal mind. He is so intent on raking straw and dust and sticks he doesn't see God."

Then they went into a sumptuous room. "What do you see here?" asked the Interpreter.

Christiana was quick to see spiders on the wall. "This shows how the ugliest creatures full of the venom of sin belong in the King's house. God has made nothing in vain."

The Interpreter went on to tell them one wise saying after another. In the morning they arose with the sun and bathed. They came out not only sweet and clean, but enlivened and strengthened. They donned fine linen, white and clean. The Interpreter called for his seal and marked their faces, so they looked like angels. And each accused the other of being fairer because they could not see their own glory.

A huge man appeared.

The Interpreter said, "Take your sword, helmet and shield, Great-Heart, and escort these pilgrims to the Palace Beautiful." And to the pilgrims he said, "Godspeed."

The pilgrims departed, singing:

"This place has been a pleasant stage,
Here we have heard and eyed
Those good things that are age to age
Hid from the evil side."

⌒

They soon came to the Cross, where Christian's burden had tumbled into the Sepulcher.

Christiana said, "Now I remember the Gate-Keeper told us we would come to the deed by which we are pardoned."

"We are redeemed from sin at a price," said Great-Heart. "And that price was the blood of your Lord, who came and stood in your place."

"My heart is ten times lighter and more joyous now," said Christiana, "yet it makes my heart ache to think He bled for me."

"You speak now in the warmth of your affection," said Great-Heart. "I hope you always will be able to."

They came upon three men hanging by the way in irons.

"Who are these men?" asked Mercy. "What did they do?"

Great-Heart answered, "They are Simple, Sloth, and Presumption. They had no intention to be pilgrims but only to hinder the pilgrims who passed by. They turned several out of the way: Slow-Pace, Short-Wind, No-Heart, Linger-after-Lust, Sleepy-Head, Dull."

Christiana said, "They got just what they deserved then."

After that they came to the Hill of Difficulty. The spring, which was once so pure, was now muddy. Great-Heart explained, "The evil ones do not want pilgrims to quench their thirst. Put it in a vessel and let the dirt settle. It will be pure again."

The two byways, Destruction and Danger, had been barred by chains, " 'The way of the sluggard is blocked...but the path of the upright is a highway,' " quoted Christiana of the wise man Solomon.

"Yet some pilgrims still take the byways," said Great-Heart, "because the Hill is very hard."

After they topped the Hill, Great-Heart gathered them beside him to walk between the lions. Suddenly a giant appeared beyond the lions.

Great-Heart called, "These are pilgrims, and this is the way they must go."

"I am Grim. Some call me Bloody-Man. This is no longer the way."

"I see now the path is overgrown with grass," said Great-Heart angrily. "You must be stopping pilgrims." He lunged at Grim with his sword. "This is the King's highway."

His sword came down on the giant's helmet and brought him down. The giant writhed on the ground, dying.

Soon Great-Heart knocked on the gate to a palace. He had only to say, "Porter, it is I," and the gate opened.

Then the pilgrims realized Great-Heart was going back to the Interpreter's house. They begged him to stay.

"I am at my Lord's command," he replied. "You should have asked him to let me go all the way with you. He would have granted your request. Good-bye."

A maiden answered the door to the palace. Upon learning Christiana was the wife of Christian, she rushed back inside where there followed the sound of rejoicing. The pilgrims received a great welcome. They met Prudence, Patience, and Charity. They feasted on lamb and ended supper with a prayer and a Psalm. Christiana asked to spend the night in the same room where her husband had slept.

"Little did I think once," said Christiana, "that I should ever follow my husband, much less worship the Lord with him."

Next morning the pilgrims sent a message back to the Interpreter's house requesting Great-Heart for their escort on the rest of the journey. While they waited, their hosts showed the apple Eve ate of, Jacob's ladder, and the very altar and knife with which Abraham was going to sacrifice Isaac. Finally Great-Heart arrived.

The pilgrims descended into the Valley of Humiliation.

"This valley is a most fruitful place," reassured Great-Heart. "See how green the valley. See how beautiful the lilies. Listen to the shepherd boy over there."

The pilgrims heard the boy sing:

"He who is down, need fear no fall;
He who is low, no pride.
He who is humble, ever shall
Have God to be his guide.
I am content with what I have,
Be it little or much:
And, Lord, yet more content I crave,
because You save such.
Fullness to those, is all a blight,
Who go on pilgrimage:
Here little, and after delight,
Is best from age to age."

Soon the pilgrims came to a pillar that read:

Let Christian's slips, before he came here,
and the battles he met with in this place be a
warning to those who come after.

"Forgetful Green here is the most dangerous place in all these parts," explained Great-Heart. "This is where pilgrims have trouble if they forget favors they have received and how unworthy they are. This is where Christian fought Apollyon. Christian's blood is on the stones to this day. Look. There are Apollyon's broken arrows. When Apollyon was beaten, he retreated into the next valley, which is called the Valley of Death."

As they entered the Valley of Death they heard groaning, as if from great torment. The ground shook and hissed. A fiend approached them, then vanished.

"Resist the devil, and he shall flee from you," remembered one of the pilgrims.

They heard a great padding beast behind them. Its every roar made the valley echo. When Great-Heart turned to face it, it too vanished. Then a great mist and darkness fell, so that they could not see. They heard the noise and rustling of the enemies.

"Many have spoken of the Valley of Death," said Christiana, "but no one can know what it means until they come into it themselves. 'Each heart knows its own bitterness, and no one can share its joy.' "

Great-Heart added, "Let us pray for light to Him who can rebuke all the devils in hell."

They continued on. Ahead of them was an old man. They knew he was a pilgrim by his staff and his clothes. The old man turned defensively.

"I am a guide for these pilgrims to the Celestial City," explained Great-Heart.

"I beg your pardon. I was afraid you were of those who robbed Little-Faith some time ago."

"And what could you have done if we had been of that company?" puzzled Great-Heart.

"Why, I would have fought so hard I'm sure you couldn't have given me the best of it. No Christian can be overcome unless he gives up himself."

"Well said," marveled Great-Heart. "What is your name?"

"My name is Honest. I only wish that was my nature." When Honest learned who the pilgrims were, he gushed to Christiana, "I have heard of your husband. His name rings all over these parts of the world for his faith, his courage, his endurance, and his sincerity."

As they walked, Honest and Great-Heart discussed a pilgrim whom they both knew: Fearing.

"What could be the reason that such a good man should be so much in the dark?" asked Honest.

"The wise God will have it so. Some must

pipe and some must weep. Though the notes of the bass are woeful, some say it is the ground of music."

As they continued on their way, they found a giant holding a man, rifling his pockets. Great-Heart attacked the giant. After the ebb and flow of much fighting, Great-Heart beheaded the giant with his sword.

Christiana asked Great-Heart, "Are you wounded?"

"A small wound, proof of my love to my Master and a means by grace of increasing my final reward."

"Weren't you afraid?" asked Christiana.

"It is my duty to distrust my own ability, so I may rely on He who is stronger than all."

"And what of you?" Christiana asked of the man Great-Heart had rescued.

"Even after the giant Slay-Good took me," said the man, "I thought I would live. For I heard that any pilgrim, if he keeps his heart pure toward the Lord, will not die by the hand of the enemy."

"Well said," agreed Great-Heart. "Who are you?"

"Feeble-Mind." He seemed reluctant to

continue on the way with the others. "You are all lusty and strong. I will be a burden." Just then a man approached on crutches. "And what of him?"

"I am committed to comfort the feeble-minded, and to support the weak," said Great-Heart.

And they all went on. At Vanity they passed through the fair. Some people even rejoiced when they learned Christiana was the wife of the famous pilgrim Christian.

They passed the hill of Lucre where the Silver-Mine claimed By-Ends and others. They passed the Pillar of Salt that had been Lot's wife. Beyond the River of God they came to By-Path Meadow where the stile led to Doubting Castle. Great-Heart halted at the warning left by Christian.

"I have a commandment to 'fight the good fight of the faith.' And who is a greater enemy of faith than the giant Despair?" Suddenly Great-Heart led the others off the way and over the stile to find Doubting Castle.

Despair rushed out, yelling, "Who are you?"

"Great-Heart, one of the King's protectors for pilgrims to the Celestial City. Prepare yourself for battle."

"I have conquered angels," bragged Despair.

Yet Great-Heart assaulted him so savagely, Diffidence came out to help. Honest cut her down with one blow. Despair fought hard, with as many lives as a cat, but died when Great-Heart cut off his head. It took the pilgrims seven days to destroy the castle. Yet Great-Heart warned:

"Though Doubting Castle is demolished,
And the giant Despair has lost his head,
Sin can rebuild the castle, make it remain,
And make Despair the giant live again."

ॐ·

When the pilgrims reached the Delectable Mountains, they were welcomed by the shepherds Knowledge, Experience, Watchful, and Sincere. The pilgrims feasted, then rested for the night. The next morning, with the mountains so high and the day clear, the shepherds showed them many things. On one mountain they saw Godly-Man, clothed in white, being pelted with dirt by two men, Prejudice and Ill-Will. The dirt would not stick to his clothes. On another mountain a man cut clothes for the poor from a roll of cloth, yet the roll of cloth never got smaller.

The pilgrims left, singing. Along the way was a man with sword drawn and face bloody. "I am Valiant-for-Truth," he said. "I was set upon by three men: Wild-Head, Inconsiderate, and Pragmatic. They gave me three choices: become one of them, go back on the way, or die. I fought them for hours. They fled when they heard you coming."

"Three to one?" marveled Great-Heart.

" 'Though an army besiege me, my heart will not fear,' " replied Valiant-for-Truth.

"Why did you not cry out?"

"Oh, I did—to my King."

They now walked the Enchanted Ground, where the air made them drowsy. Then a great darkness fell over them. They walked blindly. Thorns tore them, bushes tripped them, and they lost shoes in the mud. All about them was mud, purposely made to smother pilgrims. Yet with Great-Heart leading and Valiant-for-Truth bringing up the rear, they made their way.

They reached an arbor, warm and cozy. A soft couch was there for weary bones. Great-Heart warned them, however, that it was temptation, a trap. At the next arbor they found two men, Careless and Too-Bold, fast asleep. They could not be awakened. The Enchanted Ground was very deadly because it was so near Beulah that pilgrims thought they were at last safe.

They came upon a man on his knees. Honest knew him. "He is Standfast, a right good pilgrim. What happened, Standfast?"

"A woman of great beauty came to me. She spoke soothingly and smiled at the end of every sentence. She offered me her body, her purse, and her bed. I am very lonely, I am very poor, and I am very weary, but I turned her down several times. And yet she persisted: if only I would let her rule me, she said, she would make me so happy. She said she is the mistress of the world, Madam Bubble. I fell to my knees as you see me now and prayed to Him above who could help me. She only just left me."

"She is a witch," said Great-Heart. "It is her sorcery that enchants this ground. Anyone who lays his head down on her lap lays it on the chopping block."

The pilgrims trembled, yet sang for joy:

"What danger is the pilgrim in?
How many are his foes?
How many ways there to sin, no living
*   mortal knows.*
Some do escape the ditch, yet can fall
*   tumbling in the mire.*
Some though they shun the frying pan,
*   do leap into the fire!"*

∽

After this, they came into the land of Beulah, where sun shines night and day.

One day a messenger came to Feeble-Mind. The Master wanted him to cross the river to the Celestial City. The entire company went with him to the river. His last words as he entered the river were, "Welcome, life." Honest departed next. His last words were, "Hold out, faith and patience." As he departed, Christiana said, " 'Here is a true Israelite, in whom there is nothing false.' I wish you a fair day and a dry river when you set out for the Celestial City, but as for me, come wet or dry, I long to go." One by one over the weeks the pilgrims left. Valiant-for-Truth said, "Death, where is your sting?" as he entered the river, then, "Grave, where is your victory?" as he crossed over.

One day a messenger brought Christiana a letter:

Hail, good woman! I bring you tidings: the Master calls for you, and expects you to stand in His presence, clothed in Immortality.

As she entered the river, she said, "I come, Lord, to be with You, and bless You." Behind her, her children wept, but Great-Heart clashed the cymbal for joy. It would be many many years before the Lord called for Christiana's sons, who would take wives and greatly increase the church in Beulah.

Inspirational Library

Beautiful purse/pocket size editions of Christian classics bound in flexible leatherette. These books make thoughtful gifts for everyone on your list, including yourself!

The Bible Promise Book   Over 1000 promises from God's Word arranged by topic. What does God promise about matters like: Anger, Illness, Jealousy, Love, Money, Old Age, and Mercy? Find out in this book!
>   Flexible Leatherette $3.97

Daily Light   One of the most popular daily devotionals with readings for both morning and evening.
>   Flexible Leatherette $4.97

Wisdom from the Bible   Daily thoughts from Proverbs which communicate truths about ourselves and the world around us.
>   Flexible Leatherette $4.97

My Daily Prayer Journal   Each page is dated and features a Scripture verse and ample room for you to record your thoughts, prayers, and praises. One page for each day of the year.
>   Flexible Leatherette $4.97

Available wherever books are sold.
Or order from:

Barbour Publishing, Inc.
P.O. Box 719
Uhrichsville, OH 44683
http://www.barbourbooks.com

If you order by mail add $2.00 to your order for shipping.
Prices subject to change without notice.